One day when I was barely three a dinosaur came to play with me.

To my husband Adam, my rock.
Lurv you more!

And to my children Alaina and
Austin, it's a privilege to see the
world through your eyes. You're
my best…

About the Author

Angela Ayd is an author and photographer from Maryland. Angela loves sharing her passion and creativity in a relatable way.

He came for my
birthday filled up
with air.

And he zoomed through the house...

Over here...

Over there...

My sister took him, ran, and zipped right out the door.

And he did something
he hadn't quite done
before.

He started to float away, up, up in the sky.

I just couldn't reach him.

He was too high.

Higher he went over houses and soon...

It seemed to me he was as high as the moon!

My dinosaur was an astronaut in outer space!

And there he remains. He floats…and he waits…

My dinosaur now watches

over me.

Because I loved him...

and he loved me!

The End

Made in the USA
Middletown, DE
20 November 2020